M000040535

The Masterpiece

by Tevon Marshall
illustrated by F. Sofo

Orlando Boston Dallas Chicago San Diego

Visit *The Learning Site!*
www.harcourtschool.com

Ms. Morris couldn't wait to show her students the new sculpture exhibit. It was mentioned in all the newspapers. An amazing ancient sculpture had just been discovered. Now it was on display for the public to see.

Ms. Morris led the class up the steps and through the front door of the museum. Maria Santiago and her friend Paula trotted right behind their teacher.

Inside, Ms. Morris spotted a guard at the information desk. "How do I find the sculpture exhibit?" she asked.

The guard pointed down the hall to the left.

"I want my students to see the new sculpture right away!" she said.

The guard muttered something under his breath about people rushing around the museum. Only Maria was close enough to hear him. He continued to mutter as the class headed for the exhibit.

Ms. Morris took off down the hall. Maria, Paula, and the other students rushed after her, trying to keep up. Stuart, who was right behind Maria, whispered, "They should have given us roller skates at the information desk." Maria and Paula giggled.

The class entered the sculpture hall. Ms. Morris led the students straight to a sculpture in the center of the room. They all gathered around their teacher. "Class," said Ms. Morris, "this is the sculpture I've been telling you about. It's a masterpiece. I want you to get a good look at it."

When Maria arrived at school the next morning, she got the surprise of her life. Ms. Morris had brought the morning newspaper to class. There on the front page was a big headline: "ART THIEVES CAUGHT!"

Ms. Morris read the news article to the class. It said that a gang of art thieves had stolen the real sculpture two nights ago. The art thieves had used a very clever plan. They had replaced the real sculpture with a copy. The guard Maria had overheard was involved in the theft!

The news article said, “A student named Maria Santiago alerted the museum curator. At first, he wasn’t sure what to think of her observation. Then he checked his records. He found that the guard she had overheard had not been hired by the museum. The curator called the police. When the police talked to the guard, he didn’t have an alibi. He admitted his guilt and told them everything. He also said that the gang of thieves was planning another art robbery. Thanks to Maria’s help, one crime was solved and another was prevented.”

The article went on. "With the help of the guard, it didn't take the police long to track down the other art thieves. Luckily, they still had the real sculpture. If it were not for Maria Santiago, these thieves might have gotten away with their crime." The whole class cheered for Maria. Maria blushed and looked down at her lap.

Ms. Morris looked up from the newspaper. "Good work, Maria!" she exclaimed. All of the students clapped, even Stuart. For once, he couldn't think of anything clever to say. Ms. Morris said, "This is a special day, class. This afternoon, we are going back to the museum. There is a certain sculpture that I want you all to see."